PLAYMAKER
BILIN

The
LINEBACKER
El apoyador

by Madison Capitano
and Pablo de la Vega

Rourke
Educational Media

A Division of
Carson
Dellosa
Education

rourkeeducationalmedia.com

ROURKE'S
SCHOOL to HOME
C O N N E C T I O N S
BEFORE AND DURING READING ACTIVITIES

Before Reading: *Building Background Knowledge and Vocabulary*

Building background knowledge can help children process new information and build upon what they already know. Before reading a book, it is important to tap into what children already know about the topic. This will help them develop their vocabulary and increase their reading comprehension.

Questions and Activities to Build Background Knowledge:

1. Look at the front cover of the book and read the title. What do you think this book will be about?
2. What do you already know about this topic?
3. Take a book walk and skim the pages. Look at the table of contents, photographs, captions, and bold words. Did these text features give you any information or predictions about what you will read in this book?

Vocabulary: *Vocabulary Is Key to Reading Comprehension*

Use the following directions to prompt a conversation about each word.

- Read the vocabulary words.
- What comes to mind when you see each word?
- What do you think each word means?

Vocabulary Words:		Palabras del vocabulario	
• ballcarrier	• pursue	• captura	• perseguir
• end zone	• quarterback	• intercepción	• portador del balón
• interception	• sack	• mariscal de campo	• zona de anotación

During Reading: *Reading for Meaning and Understanding*

To achieve deep comprehension of a book, children are encouraged to use close reading strategies. During reading, it is important to have children stop and make connections. These connections result in deeper analysis and understanding of a book.

 Close Reading a Text

During reading, have children stop and talk about the following:

- Any confusing parts
- Any unknown words
- Text to text, text to self, text to world connections
- The main idea in each chapter or heading

Encourage children to use context clues to determine the meaning of any unknown words. These strategies will help children learn to analyze the text more thoroughly as they read.

When you are finished reading this book, turn to the next-to-last page for **After Reading Questions** and an **Activity**.

Table of Contents

Índice

Size, Strength, and Speed

They are strong and fast. Linebackers stop the other team from moving to the **end zone**.

end zone (end zohn): the part of a football field at each end; the area a team must reach to score a touchdown

— — — — — — — — — — —

Tamaño, fuerza y velocidad

Son fuertes y veloces. Los apoyadores evitan que los jugadores del equipo contrario lleguen a la **zona de anotación**.

zona de anotación: la parte del campo de fútbol americano que está en cada extremo; el área a la que debe llegar cada equipo para anotar

Linebackers get into position before the play.

Los apoyadores toman sus lugares antes de que comience el juego.

Linebackers are the heart and soul of a team's defense. They play behind the defensive line. Linebackers go after the **ballcarrier**.

ballcarrier (BAWL-kar-ee-ur): a football player carrying the ball on offense

— — — — — — — — — — —

Los apoyadores son el corazón y el alma de la defensa de cada equipo. Juegan detrás de la línea defensiva. Los apoyadores persiguen al **portador del balón**.

portador del balón: un jugador de fútbol americano que tiene el balón en la ofensiva

Hut, Hut, Hike!
The National Football League (NFL) was created in 1920. There were only 10 teams. Now, there are 32 teams.

— — — — — — — —

¡Hut, Hut, Hike!
La Liga Nacional de Fútbol Americano (NFL, pos sus siglas en inglés) fue fundada en 1920. Había sólo 10 equipos. Ahora hay 32.

Linebacker Luke Kuechly tackles the ballcarrier.

El apoyador Luke Kuechly taclea al portador del balón.

8

Linebackers are big. They tackle ballcarriers who break through the line. They **pursue** and catch the ballcarrier.

pursue (pur-SOO): to follow or chase someone to catch them

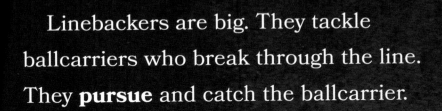

Los apoyadores son grandes. Taclean a los portadores del balón que hayan cruzado la línea defensiva. **Persiguen** y atrapan a quien lleve el balón.

perseguir: seguir a alguien para atraparlo

Inside Linebackers

Defensive formations change. Some use three linebackers. Some use four linebackers. There are inside linebackers and outside linebackers.

- - - - - - - - -

Apoyadores medios

Las formaciones defensivas cambian. Algunas tienen tres apoyadores. Otras tienen cuatro. Hay apoyadores interiores y apoyadores exteriores.

By the Book
Football playbooks can be as big as dictionaries. The team must know all of the plays. They must remember them during the game!

- - - - - - -

De memoria
Los libros de jugadas de fútbol americano parecen grandes diccionarios. El equipo debe conocer todas las jugadas. ¡Tienen que recordarlas durante el juego!

Middle linebackers are inside linebackers. They try to tackle the ballcarrier. This position covers the field from side to side.

Los apoyadores medios son apoyadores interiores. Intentan taclear al portador del balón. Esta posición abarca el campo de lado a lado.

Inside linebacker Bobby Wagner chases the running back. ▶

El apoyador interior Bobby Wagner atrapa a un corredor.

13

Middle linebackers listen to their coaches' plans. They explain it to their teammates. They lead the defense on the field.

— — — — — — — — — —

Los apoyadores medios escuchan los planes de su entrenador. Lo explican a sus compañeros. Lideran la defensa en el campo.

Star Power
The middle linebacker is called the **quarterback** of the defense. They are strong leaders. It is an important position.

quarterback (kwor-tur-BAK): player who leads the offense by throwing the ball or handing it to a runner

— — — — — — — —

Poder estelar
Al apoyador medio se le conoce como el **mariscal de campo** de la defensa. Son líderes fuertes. Es una posición importante.

mariscal de campo: jugador que lidera la ofensiva lanzando el balón o entregándolo a un corredor

Middle linebacker Sean Lee stands in a huddle. ▶

El apoyador medio Sean Lee en reunión con su equipo.

Outside Linebackers

Linebackers must think fast. They avoid blocks and watch for changes on the field.

- - - - - - - - - - - - - - -

Apoyadores exteriores

Los apoyadores deben pensar rápido. Evitan bloqueos y observan cambios en el campo.

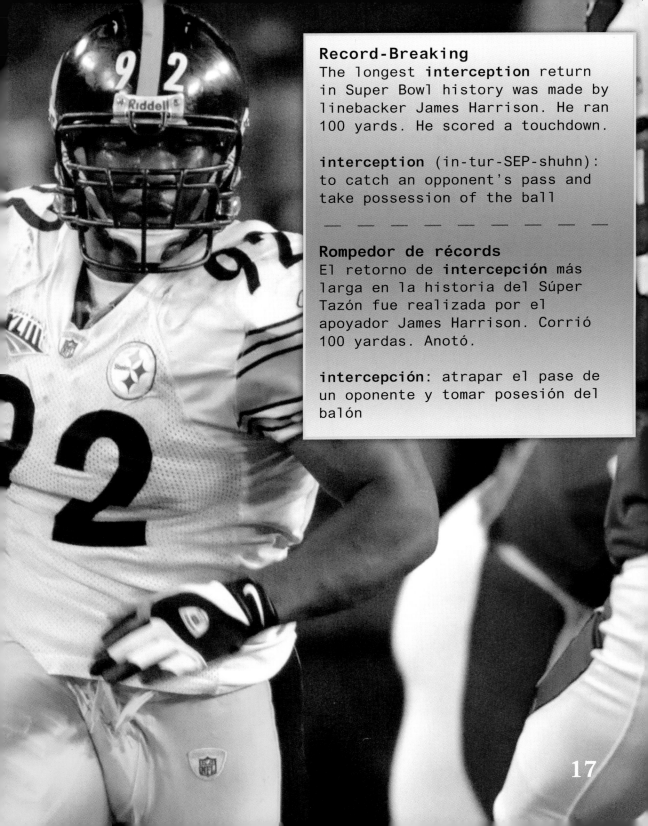

Record-Breaking
The longest **interception** return in Super Bowl history was made by linebacker James Harrison. He ran 100 yards. He scored a touchdown.

interception (in-tur-SEP-shuhn): to catch an opponent's pass and take possession of the ball

— — — — — — — — — —

Rompedor de récords
El retorno de **intercepción** más larga en la historia del Súper Tazón fue realizada por el apoyador James Harrison. Corrió 100 yardas. Anotó.

intercepción: atrapar el pase de un oponente y tomar posesión del balón

Outside linebackers watch one side, or corner, of the field. They change directions quickly. Outside linebackers have fast reactions.

- - - - - - - - - - - - -

Los apoyadores exteriores cuidan un lado del campo. Cambian de dirección rápidamente. Los apoyadores exteriores reaccionan rápido.

Outside linebacker Terrell Suggs has over 800 tackles to his name in the NFL. ▶

El apoyador exterior Terrell Suggs cuenta con más de 800 tacleadas a su nombre en la NFL.

Outside linebackers put pressure on the passer. They force the ballcarrier toward tacklers. They often **sack** the quarterback!

sack (sak): to tackle the quarterback behind the line of scrimmage

– – – – – – – – – – – – –

Los apoyadores exteriores presionan a los pasadores. Fuerzan al portador del balón a ir hacia los tacleadores. ¡Con frecuencia **capturan** al mariscal de campo!

capturar: taclear al mariscal de campo detrás de la línea de golpeo

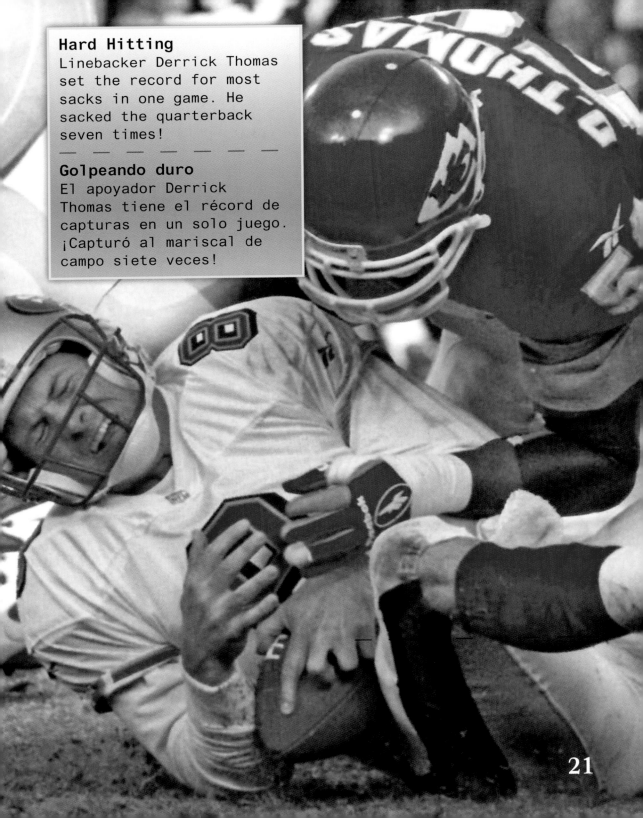

Hard Hitting
Linebacker Derrick Thomas set the record for most sacks in one game. He sacked the quarterback seven times!

— — — — — — —

Golpeando duro
El apoyador Derrick Thomas tiene el récord de capturas en un solo juego. ¡Capturó al mariscal de campo siete veces!

21

So You Want to Be a Linebacker?

Prepare for hits! Linebackers make many tackles. They get knocked down a lot too. They must practice safe tackling.

- - - - - - - - - - - -

¿Así que quieres ser apoyador?

¡Prepárate a recibir golpes! Los apoyadores taclean mucho. También son derribados seguido. Deben practicar un tacleo seguro.

Safety First

Football players must wear helmets. It is an important rule. This is good for linebackers' safety.

─ ─ ─ ─ ─ ─ ─ ─ ─ ─ ─ ─

La seguridad ante todo

Los jugadores de fútbol americano deben usar cascos. Es una regla importante. Es bueno para la seguridad de los apoyadores.

23

Learning the rules of the game is important. Linebackers can pick up a fumbled ball. They can intercept a pass. They can score touchdowns.

Aprender las reglas del juego es importante. Los apoyadores podrían atrapar un balón suelto. Pueden interceptar un pase. Pueden anotar.

Outside linebacker Telvin Smith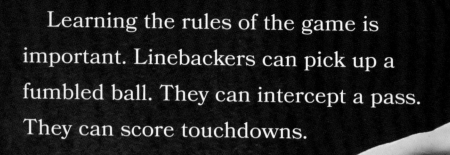
scores a touchdown.

*El apoyador exterior Telvin Smith
hace una anotación.*

24

Teamwork is important. Linebackers work together to stop the other team.

— — — — — — — — —

El trabajo en equipo es importante. Los apoyadores trabajan en conjunto para detener al equipo contrario.

Fame and Football
There are at least 30 linebackers in the Pro Football Hall of Fame. They are called *Hall of Famers*.

— — — — — — —

Fama y fútbol americano
Hay al menos 30 apoyadores en el Salón de la Fama del Fútbol Americano Profesional. Se les conoce como *Los famosos del salón*.

Outside linebackers Khalil Mack (52) ▶ and Leonard Floyd (94) try to take down the ballcarrier.

Los apoyadores exteriores Khalil Mack (52) y Leonard Floyd (94) intentan derribar al portador del balón.

Do you like action that is rough and tough? Are you fast and strong? Do you think on your feet? If you answered yes, you might make a great linebacker!

– – – – – – – – – – –

¿Te gusta la acción ruda y dura? ¿Eres veloz y fuerte? ¿Piensas con rapidez? Si respondiste que sí, ¡podrías ser un gran apoyador!

29

Memory Game / Juego de memoria

Look at the pictures. What do you remember reading on the pages where each image appeared?

Mira las imágenes. ¿Qué recuerdas haber leído en las páginas donde aparece cada imagen?

After Reading Questions

1. What are the three types of linebackers?
2. What can linebackers do with the football?
3. What is the middle linebacker sometimes called?
4. When could a linebacker score a touchdown?
5. Who do linebackers try to tackle?

Preguntas posteriores a la lectura

1. ¿Cuáles son los tres tipos de apoyadores?
2. ¿Qué pueden hacer los apoyadores con el balón?
3. ¿Cómo se le llama a veces al apoyador medio?
4. ¿Cuándo podría un apoyador anotar?
5. ¿Por qué los apoyadores intentan taclear?

Activity

Imagine you are a middle linebacker. You and the coach are coming up with a play to win the game! Name your winning plan and draw a diagram of it using different colors for the different teams.

Actividad

Imagina que eres un apoyador medio. ¡El entrenador y tú están creando una jugada para ganar el partido! Dale un nombre a tu plan ganador y dibuja un diagrama de él usando distintos colores para cada equipo.

About the Authors

Madison Capitano is a writer in Columbus, Ohio. She loves to garden, to travel, and to cook new things. Madison used to read books to her little brother and sister all the time. Now she loves to write books for other kids to enjoy.

Pablo de la Vega wasn't big on sports when he was a kid, but, oh, he loved reading books. Now he watches soccer from time to time when his friends invite him to and loves taking very long walks in cities and in nature. He sometimes translates books for children or finds who can translate them around the world.

www.rourkeeducationalmedia.com

PHOTO CREDITS: Cover: ©Thomas J. Russo; pages 4-5: ©Ric Tapia/Icon Sportswire; pages 6-7, 10-11: ©Debby Wong/Shutterstock; pages 8-9: ©Jeff Siner/TNS/Newscom; pages 12-13: ©Kirby Lee/USA Today Sports; pages 14-15: ©Ray Carlin; pages 16-17: ©Scott A. Miller/ZumaPress; pages 18-19: ©Robin Alam/Icon Sportswire; pages 20-21: ©Timothy J. Jones; page 23: ©Action Sports Photography/Shutterstock; pages 24-25: ©Jasen Vinlove; pages 26-27: ©Chris Sweda/TNS/Newscom; pages 28-29: ©NYCshooter

Edited by: Kim Thompson
Cover design by: Kathy Walsh
Interior design by: Rhea Magaro-Wallace
Translation to Spanish: Pablo de la Vega
Spanish-language edition: Base Tres

Library of Congress PCN Data

The Linebacker (El apoyador) / Madison Capitano and Pablo de la Vega
(Playmakers in Sports (Jugadores clave en los deportes))
ISBN 978-1-73162-886-2 (hard cover)
ISBN 978-1-73162-885-5 (soft cover)
ISBN 978-1-73162-887-9 (e-Book)
ISBN 978-1-73163-353-8 (e-Pub)
Library of Congress Control Number: 2019945506

Rourke Educational Media
Printed in the United States of America,
North Mankato, Minnesota